In loving memory of my precious nephew,

Christopher Michael Damman

October 11, 1982-June 6, 2011

For my wonderful grandchildren: Taylor, Chase, Gavin, Kailey, Sophia, Autumn, Audley, Georgia, Emily, Gabrielle, and Jordan.

Special Thanks to my husband, Ken, who has supported and encouraged me every step of the way throughout this project.

It was Coral's first day at Appleton Elementary School. She was very nervous, but her teacher, Miss Robbins, smiled at her warmly. "Class, this is Coral. Please help her feel welcome on her first day of school."

Miss Robbins looked down at Coral and pointed to an empty desk. "You can sit beside Samantha," she said with a smile. Coral slowly walked down the row of desks to sit beside Samantha. "Hi," whispered Samantha. "Do you want to play with me at recess?" Coral quickly nodded and then turned to face the teacher.

Samantha seems so nice, thought Coral as she tried to pay attention to what Miss Robbins was saying. She peeked around the room at some of the other kids, and then she spotted a tall, slender girl sitting in the back of the room all by herself. She had red hair in braids and lots and lots of freckles. She saw that the girl was glaring at her.

"Who's that?" she whispered to Samantha while nodding her head in the direction of the red-haired girl.

"That's Mean Jean," said Samantha. "You better stay away from her. She doesn't like anybody, least of all new kids." Coral gulped hard and then nervously peeked toward the girl again. She was still glaring at her.

At twelve o'clock Miss Robbins said, "Class, first we will have lunch, then recess." As the class began to line up to get their lunches, Mean Jean pushed her way past the others, knocking Coral off balance as she passed. She stuck her tongue out at Coral as she brushed by her.

"See what I mean," said Samantha. "Stay away from Mean Jean. Everybody in the class does!"

Coral and Samantha continued to the lunchroom and got their lunch trays. "Over here!" shouted a brown-haired boy sitting at a table with several other students.

"Come on, Coral," said Samantha. "I'll introduce you to the others."

Coral followed Samantha to the table where he was sitting. "This is Christopher," Coral said as she pointed to the brown-haired boy. "That's Katie, Kristy, and Ashley. This is Michael and Eddy. Everybody, this is Coral."

The children settled in at the table and started eating their lunches. As they were talking and laughing, Coral noticed Mean Jean sitting a few tables away all by herself. She was staring at all of them. Christopher saw Coral watching her and said, "You better stay away from Mean Jean. She doesn't like anybody!"

"Yeah, I heard," Coral whispered anxiously. "She makes me nervous." The friends went back to eating and joking around. Coral forgot all about Mean Jean as she joined in the conversation with her new friends.

After lunch, they all went outside on the playground. "Let's play basketball," shouted Katie and Kristy. "We brought our ball today."

Everybody thought that sounded like a great idea. Katie ran to get the ball from her locker, but then she noticed that Mean Jean was standing near the hoop, bouncing a blue basketball. "Hey," said Katie. "That's my ball."

"You want it?" sneered Mean Jean. She put the ball on the ground and then sat on it. "Come and get it!"

"I'm telling Miss Robbins," said Kristy.

"Go ahead, tattletale!" said Mean Jean as she picked up the ball. She started dancing around with it, singing, "Tattletale Kristy, Tattletale Kristy!"

"Aw, just forget about it, Kristy," said Christopher. "We don't want to play basketball that much anyway."

The bell rang soon, and everyone went back into the classroom. It was hard for Coral to concentrate on anything that afternoon. She kept thinking about Mean Jean and why she hated everybody so much.

That night after dinner, she went in to talk to her grandfather. "Well, Coral," he said, "how was your first day of school?" Coral sat on the sofa beside her grandfather and told him all about Miss Robbins, Samantha, Christopher, Katie, Kristy, Ashley, Michael, and Eddy. Then she looked down at the floor.

"What's wrong, my Coral?" asked her grandfather.

Coral took a deep breath and then told Grandpa all about Mean Jean and the problems they had had with her at school that day.

"Why is she so mean, Grandpa?" wailed Coral.

Grandpa thought a minute, and then he told Coral a secret about bullies. "Bullies are just people like us, only they don't feel too good about themselves. They pick on others to make themselves look bigger and stronger. I bet if she had a friend, she wouldn't be so mean."

Coral thought about what Grandfather had said as she got ready for bed that night. Then she had a wonderful idea!

The next day when Coral entered the classroom, Mean Jean was already in the back of the room. She walked down the aisle past her seat and stood in front of Jean. "Hi, Mean Jean," said Coral. Then she turned around and sat back down in her seat next to Samantha.

"Do you have a death wish or something?" whispered Samantha.

"Nope," Coral whispered back. "Just a plan."

At lunch, they all sat at their table. Coral looked around for Mean Jean and spotted her sitting in the same place she had been in the day before. And, just like the day before, Mean Jean was all by herself, scowling at everybody around her.

Coral walked over to the table and said, "Hi, Mean Jean, do you want to have lunch with us?" Mean Jean looked up at Coral, and for an instant, her scowl turned into a look of surprise. Just as quickly, her scowl returned. She jumped up and walked out of the lunchroom, looking behind her angrily at Coral.

"Are you crazy?" shouted Christopher. "Didn't we tell you to stay away from Mean Jean? She doesn't like anybody!"

Out on the playground, the children spotted Mean Jean sitting all by herself on the basketball court. She was rolling Katie and Kristy's blue basketball around, and she looked mad at the world.

"Come on," said Coral. "We're going to get that ball back."

"Just how do you think you're going to do that?" Ashley snapped sarcastically. "Are you going to just ask her for it?"

"As a matter of fact, we are," said Coral. "Just follow me."

The others nervously followed Coral as she approached Mean Jean on the basketball court.

"Hey, Mean Jean," said Coral. "How about giving us that basketball back?"

"Why should I?" sneered Mean Jean.

"Well, if you don't give it to us, then we can't play ball," Coral replied.

Mean Jean stood up and shook her fist in Coral's face. "Come and get it if you want it, but I don't think you're brave enough."

Coral turned around and faced her friends. "My grandfather told me that the best way to handle bullies is to stick together. Do we want to play basketball today or not?"

"Yeah," exclaimed Christopher. "We have to stick together. Mean Jean, give us the ball!"

Mean Jean looked at all the other children standing in a line. Then they moved and made a circle around her. To their surprise, she started to cry.

"I just wanted to be included in your circle of friends," said Mean Jean. "Nobody likes me, and nobody ever wants to play with me!" She dropped the ball and ran away with her face in her hands.

The children looked at each other with surprise, and then Ashley said, "Hey, why don't we invite Mean Jean to play with us? I would rather have her as a friend than an enemy."

They agreed and went to find Mean Jean.

They found her sitting under the slide, wiping the tears from her face. "What do you want?" she said. "You got your stupid ball back!"

Coral stepped forward. "Jean, we want to know if you want to play basketball with us. You are so tall, I bet you're great at shooting baskets!"

"Are you serious? Do you really want to play with me?" asked Mean Jean.

"Why wouldn't we want to play with you?" Coral asked. "Everybody could use a friend or two—or eight," laughed Coral.

Mean Jean stood up and held out her hand. "Friends?" she asked.

"Friends!" they shouted. Then they laughed and ran back toward the basketball court together.

What to Do if You Are a Victim of a Bully

1. Tell an adult that you know and trust. This could be your mother, father, grandparents, aunts, uncles, teachers, or the principal at your school.

2. Friends stick together and support each other in a bullying situation.

3. True friends discourage their friends from engaging in bullying behaviors.

4. Do not fight with a bully or get into a verbal argument. This only makes matters worse. Talk nicely to the bully. If the bully realizes that they cannot intimidate you, they will leave you alone.

CPSIA information can be obtained
at www.ICGtesting.com
Printed in the USA
LVIW022049170412

278047LV00002B